Cinderella

ONCE UPON A TIME, IN A GREAT KINGDOM, a gentleman lived happily with his wife, who was sweet and good, and his pretty little daughter. But alas, one day, the gentleman's wife fell ill and died. A few years passed, and the gentleman married again, a lady who was cruel, wicked, and proud. She had two daughters who were as cruel, wicked, and proud as herself. As soon as she saw her, this wicked woman hated her husband's daughter, because the girl's goodness and kindness showed up the stupidity, pride, and laziness of her own two. The day after her wedding, the stepmother ordered the poor child to do all the hard work of the household.

She had to scour the pots, wash the dishes, and clean the floors. And she scrubbed and polished her stepmother's and her two stepsisters' rooms.

She slept at the top of the house in a
dusty old attic. To reach it she had to
climb up a narrow, ill-lit staircase. When she had finished her work, the poor
child used to sit in the chimney corner, among the cinders, where it was warm.
That was why they called her Cinderella. She enraged her stepsisters even
more, because even in rags with her untidy hair, she was a thousand times more
beautiful than these vain creatures, who spent their days looking in the mirror
and arranging their hair. Cinderella was very unhappy, but she was so brave that
she never complained.

One day, a messenger from the King announced that the Prince was going to hold a grand ball, to which all the young ladies of the kingdom were invited. During the weeks beforehand, Cinderella's stepsisters spent all their time preparing their ball gowns, which gave the poor child even more work, as she was constantly sewing and unpicking, ironing, shortening and lengthening their skirts and bodices.

"I," said the elder stepsister, "will wear my red velvet dress with the silver collar."

"I," said the other, "will wear my gold-embroidered cloak and my diamond tiara."

The two sisters forced Cinderella to be present whenever they tried on their clothes, as they knew she had very good taste.

"Would you like to go to the ball, Cinderella?" asked the younger stepsister.

"Oh! I beg you, don't make fun of me. Look at my hair and my ragged clothes."

"Cinderella is right," said the elder sister. "She would look ridiculous and put us to shame."

Almost anybody would have tried to get her own back for such an insult, but Cinderella, who was not vengeful, took even more trouble to prepare their clothes. At last the evening itself arrived and the two sisters left for the ball, dressed in lavishly embroidered gowns glittering with jewels. From the window of her miserable attic, Cinderella watched them go for as long as she could and then, when the carriage was out of sight, she burst into tears.

From her far-off country, Cinderella's fairy godmother heard her goddaughter crying. With a wave of her magic wand she arrived in the dusty attic.

"What is the matter, my gentle goddaughter?" she asked.

"Oh! Godmother, I would so love to go to the ball," Cinderella replied, in tears.

"Well, you shall go to the ball, and you will be the most beautiful woman there. Go into the garden and fetch a pumpkin."

Although she was very surprised to be asked to do this, Cinderella went out and cut a big pumpkin.

With a wave of her magic wand, the fairy turned it into a magnificent golden coach.

"Now, my pretty child, I need a rat and some mice."

Cinderella brought a big rat and six little mice
from the mousetrap. With another wave of
her magic wand, the fairy turned the mice into
six fine dapple-gray horses, and the big rat
into an elegant coachman.

"Go back out into the garden once more.
Behind the watering can you will find six brightly
colored lizards. Bring them to me," said the fairy.
And when Cinderella came back, her fairy godmother turned the reptiles into
smart footmen.

"Now you are ready to go to the ball," said the fairy, admiring the
carriage proudly.

"I don't want to abuse your kindness, dear godmother, but dressed as I am I look like a beggar."

"Oh, dear! What am I thinking of?" cried the good fairy, and she waved her wand again and again until she had turned Cinderella into the most ravishing princess. Her old shirt, full of holes, became a sparkling gold silk robe. Her hair was elegantly styled with curls and intertwined braids. Then the fairy gave Cinderella a pair of glass slippers that fitted the shape of her pretty little feet perfectly. But her fairy godmother had a word of warning for her:

"Take care, Cinderella! There is one thing you must not forget. Before the twelfth stroke of midnight you must have come home from the ball, otherwise your coach will turn back into a pumpkin, your horses back into mice, your coachman back into a rat, your footmen back into lizards, and your magnificent clothes back into rags."

With a grateful heart, the lovely Cinderella promised that she
would obey her godmother and be home by the time the
clock struck midnight. Then she stepped gracefully into
her carriage, which rolled off into the night toward
the palace and the Prince's ball.

When Cinderella entered the ballroom, there was a sudden
silence: the violins stopped playing, conversations ceased, and
dumb-struck with admiration, everyone gazed at the dazzling
beauty of this unknown lady. The Prince himself begged her to sit
in the place of honor, but then he found himself unable to utter a single
word because he was so enchanted by her. However, eventually he invited
her to dance and Cinderella did so with such grace that everyone
admired her even more. Then, very politely, she went to greet her
sisters, who did not recognize her.

Time seemed to fly by until Cinderella heard the palace clock striking eleven. Immediately, she made a graceful curtsey and left the ballroom as fast as she could. As soon as she reached home, she called upon her fairy godmother.

"How can I thank you, dear Godmother? I have just had the happiest time of my life. But I have one more thing to ask you: the Prince invited me to a second ball, which is to be held tomorrow night."

The good fairy was about to answer, when Cinderella's two stepsisters knocked at the front door. Cinderella went to open it for them, rubbing her eyes, as if she had just woken up.

"How late you are,
sisters!" she said,
stretching and yawning.
"We had a wonderful
time," said the younger
stepsister. "An unknown
princess came, who was very
pleasant to us. She obviously noticed at once
that we are the sort of people to be seen with."

"Nobody knows her name," continued the elder. "We heard that the Prince
would give everything he possesses to know who she is." Cinderella smiled
and said:

"Please sister, lend me your old yellow dress, so that tomorrow I can go to the
ball to see this beautiful princess."

"What? You go to the ball? Are you mad?" cried one.

"You'd look completely ridiculous! You would make us ashamed,"
said the other.

And sniggering together, the nasty pair went off to bed.

The next evening, Cinderella's fairy godmother waved her magic wand and produced more miracles: she turned a pumpkin into a carriage, mice into horses, a rat into a coachman, lizards into footmen. And she spent even more time than the previous evening in producing Cinderella's gown.

"Tonight you must be even more beautiful than last night," said the fairy. "Instead of curls and braids you will wear your hair loose. Your dress will be made entirely of lace. As for your shoes, you can wear the same pretty glass slippers as before."

And so Cinderella left for the ball dressed like a queen.

On the palace steps, the Prince
stood waiting impatiently. When he saw
Cinderella arriving, he thought he must be dreaming: she was
even more beautiful than he remembered. Gently, he took her
hand in his and they began dancing, twirling, and spinning,
gazing constantly into each other's eyes. Cinderella enjoyed
herself so much that she did not hear the clock strike eleven
or even half past eleven. But on the last stroke of midnight,
she tore herself out of the Prince's arms in panic and ran away
like a startled deer.

She ran as fast as she could, dashing at full speed down the great palace staircase. In her haste she lost one of her glass slippers, before she disappeared into the night. As he tried to catch up with her, the Prince found the slipper on one of the stairs. Gently he picked it up, touched it to his lips and then ordered his guards to set out in search of the beautiful unknown princess. But she had vanished completely. Cinderella arrived home out of breath, with no coach, no coachman, no horses, and no footmen, and wearing her old worn clothes. All she had left of the magnificent evening was one small glass slipper.

When her stepsisters came home from the ball, Cinderella pretended to have just woken up and asked them if they had seen the beautiful princess again.

"She did come," said the elder sister, "but she ran away without even saying goodbye when the clock struck midnight."

"She ran off so fast," continued the younger, "that she lost one of her glass slippers. The Prince picked it up and he refused to dance or even speak for the rest of the evening. He just sat gazing at the little slipper in his hands."

"He is madly in love with her," continued the eldest, "and in my opinion he will do everything he can to find her again."

Indeed, the very next morning a messenger from the King declared that the Prince would marry the girl whose foot fitted perfectly into the glass slipper. First they tried the shoe on princesses, then duchesses, then all the ladies in the kingdom, but none of them had a delicate enough foot. At last the slipper was brought to the two stepsisters, who also tried in vain to squeeze their feet into it.

"Now it is your turn," said the King's messenger, turning toward Cinderella.

"You are joking," cried the two sisters, laughing unkindly. "Cinderella is just a kitchen maid!"

"I have my orders to try the shoe on all the women in the kingdom," replied the messenger.

He knelt in front of Cinderella and offered the slipper to her. The girl slipped her foot into it and of course, the shoe fitted perfectly. Then Cinderella took the other glass slipper out of her apron pocket and showed it to her stepsisters, who were astounded.

Then the fairy godmother arrived, and with a wave of her magic wand, she turned Cinderella's rags into a dress that was even more beautiful than the previous ones. The two cruel sisters recognized the beautiful princess they had seen at the ball and they fell on their knees and begged her forgiveness. Cinderella hugged them and said she forgave them with all her heart. Then Cinderella was taken to the palace where the Prince immediately recognized his fair unknown princess. He found her more beautiful than ever, clasped her in his arms and swore to love her forever. He married her and they had many children.

Cinderella, who was as good as she was beautiful, brought her stepsisters to live at the palace too and, within a year, she married them to two of the lords at court.

This edition published in 2012 by Arcturus Publishing Limited
26/27 Bickels Yard, 151–153 Bermondsey Street,
London SE1 3HA
Copyright © 2012 Arcturus Publishing Limited

ISBN: 978-1-84858-667-3
CH002344US
Supplier 15, Date 0312, Print run 1744

Printed in China